POST'S STORY: CONVENIENT LIES & PAINFUL TRUTHS

A VIRGIL TEAM PREQUEL

BONNIE BLEVINS

CONTENTS

CHAPTER 1
EX'S AND OHS'

1220hrs
26 August 2030
SGM. Post, Jerry Bowie

Post gazed out over the parade field from his position next to his rented black full cab truck. The sun was glinting off the carefully maintained vibrant green grass that was meticulously kept at a military mandated height of two inches. It stretched out in front of him for the length of a football field and twice that to the east and west. Shade offered by a nearby black walnut tree, so old it had probably witnessed the birth of the nation, kept the sweltering heat from the midday Carolina August sun off his dark head and fatigue-covered shoulders. He watched detachedly as a nearby group of 82nd paratroopers practiced their drills.

"Well, that's one thing I don't miss about regular military duties," a gravelly voice from his left stated flatly, as he shifted his impressive weight from one foot to another. Mitch 'Heavy' Youngblood was a naturally broad-shouldered barrel of a man. Combined that with an unwavering attachment to weightlifting and he cut quite the intimidating figure.

Post shared Heavy's sentiment. It had been years since he had to take part in the normal fanfare of day-to-day military duties. Almost five years had passed since his being called on to serve as Sergeant Major of the shadowy sixth branch of the U.S military dubbed "Black Branch." A unit nothing like any in the normal military, it was more like something portrayed in a dramatic TV show, but without as many neatly tied up, happy endings. No, they were meant to go in and prevent, deter, or stop any enemy around the world be it behind enemy lines, or within their own government. They were welded to be the ultimate tip of the spear, and capable of a great deal, but even they couldn't ensure a happy ending all the time. Sometimes they had to settle for just coming home with the same number of holes they'd left with.

A chill breeze cut through the heat of the day, offering a momentary respite to all present and bringing with it a reminder of the impending fall season. Post inhaled it deeply, relishing the earthy scent unique to fall in the south. It enveloped him in memories of simpler days spent at family barbecues in Mississippi; the crunch of leaves underfoot, the smell of charcoal, and his sheer joy as he ran between his daddies' grill and the multitude of family members, friends, neighbors, and church family.

The sound of an approaching vehicle roused him from his reverie and signaled the arrival of Virgil Team's leader. He and Heavy both turned in unison to watch as the blacked-out SUV pulled up next to them. Marine Corps Master Sergeant Kale Reyes quickly stepped out, slamming the door shut behind him. Walnuts crunched under his combat boots as he crossed the short distance towards them. His bronze skin reflected the noon sun as his green digital fatigues did their job and absorbed it.

"Been awhile since I've seen you in Marine Corp issued digis, boss," Heavy's voice boomed, louder than necessary, across the open field. It drew more than a few sideways glances at the unusual trio. While Fort Bragg was home to Joint Special Operations Command, it still was abnormal to see a marine, seaman, and soldier lined up next to the command parade field. If Post was a betting man, he'd gamble there was at least a joke or two about them right now amongst the paratroopers watching them from afar.

"Back at you. Never did understand why the navy wears dark blue… how the hell do they find you when you go overboard in the damn ocean?"

"I'm a Seal, I ain't falling off shit. And if by chance I do, I'll swim back to the ship and climb back on. Why else do you think I have these guns for?" A quick flex of his generous bicep accentuated his comment.

Post shook his head in exasperation. Despite being his best team in Black Branch, he really wondered about them sometimes. Kale looked behind them, out at the parade field, and had the same look on his face that Post was sure he had worn just a moment ago. Long before any of them joined special operations, they'd all started at the bottom, on a parade field, with drill sergeants in their faces doggedly stripping them down to build them back to their full potential.

"Glad to see y'all are enjoying reminiscing."

"What exactly is 'this one' Jerry? It's not often we have to don our old uniforms for a mission… nor are you usually with us," Kale inquired, while leaning casually against the truck as he leveled his full focus on his branch's Sergeant Major.

The look would have wilted a lesser man. Kale had always been an intense individual, even before what had happened to him and his team a few years ago. After that, the man had all but frozen over, only caring about getting his team through the next mission in one piece and never taking the time to recover himself. He hoped that time would thaw his friend, but it seemed to have only buried him under more layers of ice. It seemed to him that maybe Kale just needed the right person to bring him back to them, but would he ever allow someone to get close enough to him again?

Pushing away his thoughts, he moved away from the truck and squared up with Kale before handing him the nondescript manilla folder. Kale raised an eyebrow at the hard copy being presented to him, since they usually relied so heavily on their tech guy, Guru, for distributing information digitally.

Post flexed his shoulders in a half shrug, "So sue me, I'm nostalgic… and I want this to stay off the net as much as possible." He had memorized the file and knew what Kale would see. A picture of a middle-aged female First Sergeant, and a report of an insider threat within the most secure and important military leadership group of the United States military: JSOC.

"Post… qué diablos?" Slipping into Spanish as the shock of revelations held within the damning yellow folder hit him, Post turned on his heel in an attempt to hide his reaction.

"Is this who I think it is?" Kale passed the file to Heavy as his voice exhibited his disbelief in what he'd just read. Post couldn't blame him. He'd had the exact same reaction when Guru had brought it to him, knowing of his connection to the woman and wanting to keep the find of a major leak in JSOC confined within the special operations community. It was only due to his unquestionable trust in Guru and his leads that he hadn't turned on the man and cried foul. If that file had come from anyone else in the world, he would have told them to shove it where the sun didn't shine and that there was no way in the nine hells it could be true.

Post crossed his arms then, in a base human reaction to protect himself from the harsh words his men, and friends, were about to utter to him. Normally he would hide such a tell, but he knew he didn't need to from these two. He could count on one hand how many people in this world he trusted unconditionally, and Heavy and Kale were firmly among them.

A forceful sigh escaped Heavy as he made the same connection Kale had. "Boss… is this who we think it is? And do these documents point to her in connection with these leaks? These deaths?"

Post's shoulders drooped. His head fell forward. "Yeah, that's my former fiancé. And we are here to investigate if she is the mole that Guru has uncovered within JSOC."

CHAPTER 2
JSOC

1305hrs

26 August 2030

SGM. Post, Jerry Bowie

The JSOC building was a stuffy place. One would think that those who earned a spot at the Joint Special Operations Command would loosen up a bit. *'But, No. We all have sticks up our asses the sizes of our egos,'* he thought, in an uncharacteristically snarky inner voice.

Post adjusted his dress greens once more out of agitation as he proceeded down the next hall that he had been directed towards. His own short temper was annoying him; even he could admit that. He refused, however, to acknowledge why he was agitated and why his palms, that never sweated in the heat of combat, were presently as slick as a schoolboy's at junior prom.

His shoulders ached. He rolled them. Then sharply bent his head to crack the kink forming in his neck. *'Here I thought a bullet would get me before old age, or a woman. It's all for the mission, just focus on the mission.'* He recited this new mantra in his head as he approached the secure vault door leading to the next secure section of the building.

Army Sergeant Major Jerry Bowie Post, who knew nothing but taking timely and decisive action to execute his mission, fumbled for the first time in his military career and stared dumbfounded as the heavy door opened.

She stared back. Her hazelnut eyes missed nothing. The sly Mona Lisa smile that barely cracked her face spoke to how she had caught his lapse, and she knew that would piss him off.

A knot formed around his windpipe. He swallowed more forcefully than necessary before managing a proper response, "Veronica."

"Bowie. So, you do remember how to call my name then?" There it was again, that smirk which teased at him, threatening to pull down his wall and shatter it to dust. She was the only person in the world that could get under his armor, and she absolutely loved it. It was one reason their engagement had been so short-lived.

His fidget to fix his tie, which was not off by a centimeter, bought him time to get out from under her pinning look. "Very funny V. So, you going to let me in now or are we going to pull out the rulers next?"

Veronica had worked hard to earn her place in the army, and even harder to earn her place in JSOC. It meant that she always needed to have the biggest dick in the room and be ready to measure it at any moment. He knew, in fact, that she often carried a ruler around with her. Each time a man gave her lip at a new unit, she'd hand him the ruler and spear him with that patented female glare that dared them to say another word. Usually, after the first week or so, she wouldn't need the ruler again. Then she'd go to a new unit and repeat the process all over again until the dust settled.

Her shrug of fake surrender was elegant, he thought, as she turned to the side to allow him entry to the SCIF behind her. The metal frame protecting the door to the sensitive compartmented information facility was tight with her standing here and he couldn't help but take her in again as he brushed by her.

She wasn't a small woman, and it was solely because she worked out to keep her physical strength on par with the male standard of any special ops member of her teams. Her elegant blonde hair was in a braided bun, with not a single strand awry. The latte browns of her eyes shone with humor at how she still had the ability to put him on his back foot. Red lipstick was the only trace of makeup on her; you could take a New Yorker out of New York, but she was still going to hold onto that New York City flare somehow.

Once, and only once, he'd made the mistake of calling her a "basic white woman" because of that shade of red on her lips. Her city dwelling self was equally foreign to him as his Mississippi country self was to her. Somehow that fight in the red room of their unit's building had ended with them tangled up in bed and connected at the hip for just over two years.

As he entered the secure room, he mentally reprimanded himself for letting his thoughts wander. Taking advantage of her back being to him as she shut the door, he shook his legs out, willing his suddenly too tight briefs to loosen. '*No wonder I can't think, my blood's in the wrong place.*'

Stealing himself against the drawl she always exerted over him, he reflexively blurted out, "Let's get to why I'm here."

Turning to look at him squarely, she cast a quick look behind him of obvious annoyance. It was then he realized that not only was that the most confrontational thing he could've said, but that he'd said it in a room filled with other operators, all of whom were now interested in the exchange between the two senior non-commissioned officers. His skin tightened in reaction to a feeling he hadn't had in years: embarrassment. He felt like the physical embodiment of Homer Simpson yelling "doh!"

She briskly walked past him then, tossing a slight glare over her shoulder that brought him back to their many fights five years ago. Veronica had a way of making any shoe she was wearing, whether combat boot or Ugg, sound like she was wearing five-inch Prada heels. The woman didn't walk, she strutted. It was another aspect of the undercover New Yorker that she had yet to shed. Post felt the sting of her reprimand but taking her queue, he followed behind her heel strikes so as not to air things out any further in the main room of the SCIF.

While he was embarrassed by his lapse of decorum, he refused to show it or admit to it in front of the fifteen or so military personnel in the room. While they had all gone back to their assigned duties, he remained acutely aware of a few glances being shot his way and even caught an openly disdainful look being drilled into him.

The twenty-meter walk to a well-appointed, oak panel executive office felt like the longest field of fire he had ever suffered through. Veronica swept through the room as its appointed queen and rested her toned ass against a metal table that contrasted poorly with the beautiful room it was situated in. As he stepped across the threshold, he pulled the heavy oak door shut behind him.

"What the actual Hell on Earth Jerry? What are you thinking?!"

Her voice caressed his skin like a siren's song, despite the scolding tone lacing it. *'Damn, how long has it been since I heard her voice?'* He silently pondered the thought long enough that she threw her arms up in a gesture that screamed the same words she'd just said aloud.

Annoyance flooded through him as he mentally beat his own ass for acting like a love-sick puppy. He needed to find out as covertly as possible if she was the mole in JSOC, not acting like a rookie around a former lover. "Veronica, fuck that, what's going on in your department?"

The look of cold water thrown in her face made him smile inwardly. For the first time in the last five minutes, he actually felt like Sergeant Major Jerry-Fucking-Post.

She bristled and pushed off the desk, staring at him for a moment before circling it and settling into an uncomfortable-looking chair that looked like it'd survived the Bay of Pigs invasion. As she sat down, she steepled her hands in front of her on the desk. Her eyebrows curved elegantly above her intense eyes that drilled into him.

"Why is the Sergeant Major of Black Branch here, Jerry?" her gaze was lethal, "As much as I had a small hope this was a social visit for an apology, I realize now—as usual—you are purely here on business… why?"

Ignoring her digs at him, he leaned back against the paneled wall behind him, "You have a leak in your office V… and it's a big one, one that's getting troops killed. We are here to help you plug it." He didn't know it was possible, but her fair skin turned another shade of white momentarily. Then, in a motion as quick as it was smooth, he watched as she tossed a file on top of a Zune – a digital music player that had been discontinued over twenty years before.

'*The actual-fuck, is she doing with an MP3 in a SCIF?*'

Catching his look of interest, she spoke in a forced-sounding bored tone, "It's my office, and I work better with music. That thing is too old to do anything to the systems, so IT isn't bothered by it." Her glare challenged him to question her further, but he accepted her response and returned his focus to the matter at hand.

"It's your house, V."

"Damn right it is."

Letting out an exasperated breath, he crossed the room, leaned over her desk, and slammed his palms down on her desk. Putting himself in her personal space. His goal was simple. To get a true reaction out of her to see if she was hiding something or not. He was the perfect man for this mission as he knew all of her tells intimately and knew the best way to get her to tip a hand she may have was to get her fired up.

"Enough of this, Veronica, this is serious."

She bolted upright, her brows furrowing as her mocha eyes turned a darker shade that signaled impending violence. He had been on the receiving end of that look more times than he'd like to count.

"You think I don't know that, fucker!" And there it was, her New York accent, signaling that he had utterly pissed her off. She usually smothered it well, but any southerner or northerner can only manage it so long. When their level of ticked off hits THAT level, it comes out to play. "Some'are mine that died. Now if you're here to help, good, if not, see y'r-self out."

Taking a step back from the desk, he held his arms up in the international gesture of surrender, "I'm not here to fight, V. I'm here to help you and catch this mole."

Throwing herself back into her aging relic of a chair, she huffed, "Come in 'ere and… " she began to mumble in her way that brought a smile to his face despite his attempt to remain stony-faced. He didn't want to believe Guru, but she could be the very mole they were hunting. Shaking his head, he thought, '*No, she is many things, but not a traitor. Her commitment to her country is absolute - it can't be her. The only thing she is more committed to is her son.'*

Another glare. Another long moment of silence. Then her shoulders finally relaxed, signaling the end to her ire, "What do you need?"

"I need two of my men to have access to Pope Air Force Base's runway, in some inconspicuous positions that can get them into each aircraft that lands. We have intelligence that indicates this leak may be messing up and double dipping."

She cast a sidelong glance at him as she grabbed her Zune from under the file and started flipping it over in her hands like a fidget spinner. "What do you mean… double dipping?"

"This leak is one we only found because they started a side hustle bringing in goods via C130's coming over from the Middle East. Without them getting greedy like that, the intelligence leak itself may have gone unnoticed even longer than it did." Pausing, he crossed his muscular arms across his chest stretching the green wool fabric to its limits, "Tell me you knew nothing of any of this, V."

Without warning, the chair went flying into the back wall and created such a cacophony of ear-piercing noises that he was sure it would bring the entire office of operators running. Veronica had almost vaulted over the desk as she leaned over it to get as far into his personal space as she possibly could with the desk still between them, "Really?! You think I'm a'spy? A traita'!?"

Knowing it would piss her off even more, and hoping to put her on the defense, to show him whether or not she really was a "traita'", he let his next jab fly. "I don't know, YANKEE." He drew the word out, knowing she hated being called it. "Are ya? The leak is from YOUR office right under YOUR nose. You sniffed me out on every so-called lie, but you somehow can't figure out a mole is right under YOUR nose; In YOUR unit?"

It seemed they had both stopped breathing as her complexion went from pristine white, to mad red, before landing on scarlet pissed-the-fuck-off. She was so enraged at him she genuinely couldn't find any words to hurl. Her breath had grown ragged, but between heaves she managed to choke out, "How. DARE. You. Bowie."

Then, without another word, she did something he knew would only happen in his presence—a sign she still trusted him to some degree—she dropped her façade. He watched as the weight of the world crashed into her like a wrecking ball, causing her to cave in on herself as she crumpled to the desk. Her shoulders shuddered. He knew she was doing the thing that all badass women knew how to do as easily as drawing breath: cry silently.

It was at that moment he knew she couldn't be betraying her country. This had been her genuine reaction in each of their fights back when they were a couple and had pushed each other to their breaking points to pull out a truth that they should have just spoken.

Maw-maw Renita had taught him that only two things bring out someone's true nature: love, and anger. Post and Veronica had both seen each other at their best and worst, which meant that they would always know when an emotion or reaction was genuine. It was the realest way to know if someone was lying, and Veronica's rage and subsequent moment of vulnerability had just proven to him that she was not the mole.

In a response born from being a man of action—and Veronica's former lover—he slowly walked around the desk, knelt by her side, and rubbed a soothing hand across her back. She had taught him that if a woman was crying silently, it was because she did not want to draw attention to her moment of perceived weakness in a world where crying meant you weren't capable of your job, weren't a soldier, and weren't to be respected. Crying made you a target, and women already had targets on their backs.

She began to calm under his hand. He told her then, with more emotion than intended, "I'm sorry, V, I needed to know." A small red eyed glare flashed at him from under her arm. He gave her a little smile, "You know I love making you turn colors…" with a wink, he let his innuendo hang between them in an effort to diffuse the tension he had created.

A soft giggle, then an exhausted sigh rewarded his efforts, "I know why, but I'm still pissed you did it… and I would have done the same in your shoes." Slowly, she sat up. The bags under her eyes were a little darker, and her spirit quieter from their exchange. She rotated the chair to face him in full, placing him comfortably between her knees.

Leaning over, she put her ruby tinted lips next to his ear, "Don't play with fire unless you mean it." She placed a lingering kiss right under his earlobe, right in the spot she knew hit him to the core, then backed away.

Post had to fight the urge to grab her knees and place her firmly back where she was so that he again was cradled between those luscious thighs. Clenching and unclenching his fists to reel in his desires, he watched her wearingly, torn over the feelings that had raced through him in the last ten minutes.

"V…" the pleading edge to his voice felt foreign to him. Even when they were dating, he had never begged her.

A wicked grin graced her face, full of such mischief that it made her eyes twinkle. "Take me to dinner in downtown, there is a nice cafe down the road from the Airborne and Spec-Ops Museum and then you can say my name like that again…" He watched in amazement as the walls came back up in an instant and this tender lost lover turned back to a battle hardened First Sergeant of a JSOC unit.

"In regard to your request, give me their names and have them report at 2100hrs tonight to Pope's airstrip. Those flights come in at night, so I can see why this 'double dipper' has chosen them. BUT…" her voice was clear and cut like a sharpened combat knife through the air between them, "I want updates on everything. This is my unit, my show, and nothing is to happen without my express go ahead, am I clear?"

He cast an indignant look at her, his shoulders squaring, though remaining crouched across from her, "You know I am the Sergeant Major of an entire military branch and you are not… right?"

She pursed her red lips, forming a solid formidable line as she crossed her arms pointedly and cocked her head to the side.

"If you're such a hot shot, why are you asking for my lil' ol' help then?"

They locked eyes as the government issued clock rudely announced each second's passing in the otherwise undisturbed silence before he finally gave in, "Fair point."

Standing up stiffly, due to his dress pants feeling two sizes too small in one particularly sensitive area, he started for the door. With a tense hand on the doorknob, he cast a quick look behind him, "Dinner. Twenty-hundred hours?"

"I'll meet you there."

CHAPTER 3
FOR. THE. MISSION

1411hrs
26 August 2030
SGM. Post, Jerry Bowie

His shoulders were hunched, eyes narrowed, and gait long and heavy. 'Ruffled' would describe his inner world at that moment, and he did not enjoy the feeling. She was the only person on the planet capable of jarring him out of his stoic mindset before putting him back on his feet and sending him on his way with just a few words like that.

As he breached the final door that blocked his path to freedom from the cinderblock building masquerading as something far more polished and rosy, he felt some of the tension in him diminish. Normally he would chalk up the knot in his stomach to a gut-feeling that something was wrong, and the shit was about to hit the fan, but this time he gave all the credit to his former fiancée and the embers of long dormant feelings having been stoked by their encounter.

'Has it really been five years since we've been together?' His dark thoughts clung to him like the depression he was at constant war with. Maintaining continuous vigilance was necessary to prevent it from

swamping him and dragging him into the bog of self-loathing and hatred that he knew he'd never escape from again. Roughly twenty-two active-duty military and veterans take their lives every day, and once he was almost among their ranks. It was why he made a point of making mental health services readily available to—as well as destigmatizing their use by—his warriors of Black Branch.

"Went that well, huh?"

Heavy's voice was like walking into a brick wall. It had shocked him out of his thoughts so quickly that he'd instinctively sunken into a crouch like he was hunkering down for a physical attack.

"Apparently not… it's alright, we got your six," Kale called out to him, like he was soothing a spooked horse while somehow also managing to be unpatronizing. The two men were standing next to Kale's SUV and watching him warily. Worry was etched just barely into their eye and mouth lines. It was so subtle that only those closest to the men would have noticed the change.

Annoyance again at his lapse of awareness and carelessness creeped up his spine. He gritted his teeth so hard they squeaked like nails on chalkboard in a way that would've caused most people to shudder.

"Fuck," he muttered under his breath, as he closed the distance between himself and his men, hoping that no one else had noticed his jumpiness. His body felt like it wasn't his own. A charged up, ungrounded feeling thrummed throughout his hormones and military instincts, like they had just taken a direct hit from a lightning bolt and were looking for an outlet. The vein on the side of his temple throbbed as he turned his back to the building and the infuriating woman inside it that demanded his full attention.

"I'm fine," he snapped, in a voice so terse and far-removed from his usually calm and even demeanor that it showed he was as far from fine, as 'fine' could get.

Before he let Heavy or Kale call him on his blatant lie, he issued them his orders. Pulling rank like that was a convenient way of saying he would not be talking about what had happened. He knew they would see through it, but he needed to exert some sense of control to keep himself steady.

"Get changed into digi fatigues. Get over to Pope Air Force base's landing field. You are expected to report in at 2100 hours. If Guru finds anything more, he'll send it directly to you."

His two best men exchanged uneasy looks then leveled their intense gazes on him, "And that leaves you free to do…?"

Ducking his head to conceal his face under the brim of his military cover, he begrudgingly told them, "I have dinner plans. If you find anything that could be related to this leak and these unauthorized cargo shipments, report in immediately. Don't go all Bass Reeves on me and chase a lead by yourselves." He could feel the burn of their gazes drilling into him, pressing for more information. It was information he was not going to give them.

"That's all, you're dismissed. Report in tomorrow at zero-eight-hundred-hours if nothing that requires immediate action comes up tonight." His boot heel crushed the gravel as he spun on it in a perfectly executed about-face, putting himself in the opposite direction of Heavy and Kale's inquisitive glances.

'It's for the mission. We are only having dinner - For. The. Mission.'

CHAPTER 4
COLD STEEL AND WARM FLESH

1945hrs
26 August 2030
SGM. Post, Jerry Bowie

Nerves of steel. He would have sworn he had them, that is until he was getting ready for dinner. It was his first dinner with that woman in years. Since he had broken up with her, he'd had his share of one-night stands, but he hadn't dated. He'd always known there would be no one for him but her. Loving someone with all his being was something he didn't think he had been capable of until her. She had grabbed him by the balls and never let go.

She was his everything, and he felt no desire to ever date again.

Sure, he still had needs. He was a man who believed in taking care of himself, and being celibate wasn't for him, but it didn't mean he didn't picture her swirling brown eyes, red lips, and platinum hair when he was with every single one-nighter.

It took him an obscene amount of time to get ready for 'just dinner.'

"Not a date," he said forcefully to himself, as if reprimanding his own reflection in the mirror would quell the cyclone of butterflies churning his stomach into mush.

Just as any good soldier does, Post had arrived early to her chosen spot. The Blue Moon Café was ideally positioned in downtown Fayetteville. Its blue and tan window trim was the only thing that separated the two-story brick building from the other rust-colored buildings along the street. A string of lights crisscrossing the two-lane road in front of it lent the exterior a soft illumination, creating a cozy ambiance despite being nestled along the busy main street.

Taking his eyes off his surroundings, he glanced in the visor mirror and checked himself again. *'It is for the mission... why would she want me back anyways? I always prioritized my missions over her before, it's why she left me, after all.'*

He recalled the day when he had come home to their two-bedroom apartment to find it empty. She had packed herself and her teenage son up. She'd left a note that read, *'I won't make you choose between me and my son or a mission again. But I won't be the grieving widow while raising my son through the loss of another father. I'll always love you, Bowie. Stay alive.'*

'Stay alive,' those were the same two words she'd said to him before any mission. Not that she loved him or to come back to her, but to stay alive. He had promised her the day he had asked for her hand in marriage that he would always 'stay alive,' but he had also promised to take up a new role that wouldn't require deployment to active combat zones. He didn't follow through. He couldn't at the time. Some said the action was like crack to special ops personnel. There are some operators who've done the job so long, they just don't know how to survive without knocking on death's door at least a couple times a year.

Veronica had given him two warnings.

He thought she wouldn't leave. Then she did. Now he was here.

He leaned back against the headrest and stared out the truck's sunroof. *'What A useless and dangerous feature'*, he thought, that left him exposed to a sniper from one of the taller buildings' roofs. He didn't like it, but then again—even in the relative safety of the US—he was constantly analyzing everything for threats and weaknesses.

Finding no sense of calm to soothe his storm, he gave up waiting for a suitable time to walk into the café.

He knew he would be there early, and she would be there late. She was always on New York time, which according to her was "fashionably late time" because she was getting "fashionable." As he stepped out of his rented truck, he smoothed a callused hand over his polo and fixed his jeans so they sat a little higher on his hips, shifting the weight of the concealed Glock secured in his waistband in his top-of-the-line holster.

"I always did find that annoying when hugging you from behind…"

Post spun on his heel at the sound of her voice. There she was, standing just by his truck's tail lights.

"… No woman likes cold steel where only warm flesh should be," she purred, flashing the one weapon that could disarm him without fail, her smile. It lit up his night and left him fumbling for words.

She crossed the remaining distance between them and smoothed a hand over his polo's collar before looking up into his face. The corners of her eyes tilted upwards with her grin that threatened to break into a laugh. "I always did enjoy sneaking up behind you though. Hi Bowie." With a speed that made him think he imagined it, she planted a peck on his cheek then stepped away and motioned towards the café.

"I saw you sitting there for the last ten minutes fidgeting in your truck. I figured you thought I'd be late and that's why you were trying to look like you'd gotten here at a reasonable time, rather than thirty minutes early." She raised an eyebrow at him as he snapped his jaw shut with an audible click.

'How does she do that? Always taking me off guard one minute, then schooling me the next. And damn… doesn't that red jumpsuit fit her perfectly!'

It took him longer than he would have liked, but after a couple seconds spent recovering from her unexpected presence and bombardment, he was able to find his voice.

"You've never been early for anything. I feel like I just walked into a trap."

His lips curved ever slightly as he crossed his arms over his broad chest. Trying his best to stop locking in on the generous amount of cleavage her jumpsuit revealed. She'd pulled that zipper low–he was sure–for his torture.

A flash of emotion that he couldn't place ripped across her face. Was it guilt, or shame perhaps? It was gone so quickly he was not able to analyze it any further, replaced now by a look of mock shame and indignation.

"How dare you accuse a New York lady–of all people–of setting a trap for a man!"

They both allowed genuine smiles to crack their features. He stepped forward then, to be at her side. Her shiny red heels expanded her 5'7" height to almost match even with his 6 feet.

"Then allow a humble Mississippian man from the Delta to escort the lady to dinner."

Their banter came easily, like sheet music they didn't even need to glance at. They'd played this melody a thousand times before, in another lifetime, and they fell back into the rhythm of it like they'd never stopped.

After walking arm in arm into the small boutique café, they settled into a secluded area near the back. It was an area reserved for patrons who were on quiet nights out, as it was clear the families were located towards the front and the parties of two were located more in the back. He didn't mind the assumption that they were a couple, he secretly reveled in it.

Veronica and he had seemed to pick up right where they had left off as they talked casually through dinner. This was their dynamic from back before his last deployment. Before her decision to leave him. The remnants of their dinner lay between them as they both leaned back into their cushioned metal café seats and sipped their chosen drinks. He had paid less mind to his phone over the last few hours then he should have, considering his team was running reconnaissance, but trusted in his tech man Guru's ability to reach him if shit hit the proverbial fan.

"How is John-Masters?" he probed casually, as they finished discussing current affairs. He had been avoiding bringing up her son until that moment; a boy who would have been his stepson, had things gone differently.

Veronica leaned back into her chair and he watched as an unseen weight settled down on her, "John…" she shook her head and gave a small unenthusiastic laugh, "He did what we both asked him not to do."

"He enlisted?"

"Yup," she said softly, then looked down and held up a hand before he could ask the next obvious question, "Army, of course, and to answer the next one, for reasons known only to him, he joined the MP corps."

His eyebrows shot up as he took in the new information. "Like his father?"

Her eyes glazed over momentarily at the mention of John's father. He had been only a casual friend with benefits for Veronica, but they had married after learning that she was pregnant. However, he went MIA on his last mission and had been missing for the past twelve years. There were theories about what had happened to him, but none were ever substantiated. Post knew Veronica had not been in love with the man, but he held a special place in her heart as John's father.

"Yeah, I guess he thought he could start his military career off on a similar path as him. He's running into trouble, though."

He wasn't able to prevent the smile which tugged at the corners of his lips from spreading . He may have only lived with, and raised, John-Masters for a couple of years, but even in that time he'd learned how strong-willed and stubborn the boy was. "What kind of trouble?"

Veronica leaned forward again, smiling back, "The kind you and his father would have gotten into; standing up for what he believed in, but doing so with a senior non-com. Though I hear he has a rather…" she paused, as if weighing what words to use, "Intuitive, Staff Sergeant, that I think will support him in navigating this stumbling block. He never was one to care about authority figures," she giggled, in that endearing way women have perfected to capture a mate's attention, "Don't we both know that to be true with him?" She laid a hand gently on his that'd been fondling his empty rum glass. "He still asks about you, ya know?"

"Does he?" He squeaked back, instantly embarrassed by his less than masculine tone. He attempted to hide any vulnerability beneath a deeply furrowed brow, but the corner of his mouth involuntarily twitched.

"I'd be lying if I said I did not keep tabs on him myself." His shoulders raised slightly at her surprised look. "What? If you want me to st-"

Her hand squeezed his, "No. No. I appreciate it, he needs the extra set of eyes on him... especially now." The last few words he had almost missed as she had said it so low. He wanted to question her about it, but her hand had started to draw circles on the back of his.

"Veronica..." his voice sounded hoarse and limp as his logical inner voice barked at him '*For. The. Mission.*'

She leaned over the table then, the zipper of her jumpsuit leaving an impression along the top of her bosom that begged for him to free it from his confinement. As he forced himself to break his attention from the delicate flesh and its cry for him to save it, he found her giving him that knowing smile of hers that told him she knew exactly what he was thinking. Before he could give some excuse for his boyish lingering stare, she placed a single delicate finger under his chin. With just a slight amount of pressure, she lifted his head, gave him her trademark smile, then went in for the kill. The kiss was tender, sweet, and filled with an urge to satisfy a dormant longing that suddenly rose up within them both. Before that moment, he would have bet every medal on his chest that she would never want him again. It was a good thing he wasn't, as his dress uniform would have been bare.

She gave him all the answers to every question he had ever wondered since they'd parted ways, and he'd seen her again that morning, with just that single lingering kiss.

'*Could she ever want me again?*'

Her tongue followed the bow in this upper lip. Yes.

'Does she miss me?'

She nipped his bottom lip. Yes.

'Could I ever show her how much I've truly longed for her?'

His tongue darted past her lips and hers mated with it. Yes.

'Can she ever love me again?'

Breathing was forgotten as she wrapped a hand around the base of his neck and tugged ever so slightly. *'Maybe, just mayb—'* His hopeful thoughts were rudely interrupted as an annoying stock phone ringtone made them both jump in each other's arms and stare at her offending device.

"I-I-I'm sorry Bowie, I…" her cheeks were turning cherry blossom pink, "I shouldn't have gotten carried away like that, not tonight." Again, he noticed that she mumbled the last part as she pocketed her phone without looking at the offending intruder's message.

Taking a moment to tug at the area tightening in his pants, he tried to gather his thoughts after having his mind scattered to the winds. It took him a moment longer than it normally would to notice the change in the woman sitting across from him.

Those desire-tinged cheeks from only moments ago were gone, along with the eyes that'd been so full of sweet-nightlong-promises. In their place were the rigid features of a soldier with a mission.

Immediately, he matched her energy and went on high alert and checked his phone to see if he had missed an update from his team. When he found nothing waiting for him, he returned his attention to her, "What happened?"

Her eyes narrowed, and he saw her take a deep breath before glancing out the large windows of the café. "I need to go, Jerry, I'm sorry," she said wistfully, keeping her gaze directed out into the night.

It had grown late, he realized, as he caught the time on the clock above the door. 2346hrs. That explained why there were only a few patrons, mostly couples, and just two staff still present.

"Why are you sorry?" His eyebrow instinctively rose as he cocked his head to the side. Curious then as her use of certain words throughout the night came unbidden to his mind, the ones she had mumbled under her breath thinking he hadn't heard her. His gut flipped, and for the first time since seeing her that morning he didn't attribute it to some lovesick feeling. This feeling was one that had saved him in life or death situations.

The look she gave him only made that feeling even worse, "Just know I am, Bowie..." she trailed off, slid her metal chair across the concrete floor of the café, rose from her seat with purpose, then paused for a moment to ask a question without looking at him, "Walk a girl to her car?"

Alarm bells screamed in his head, her entire body language had changed with the ringing of that phone, why? His gut told him '*No*', but his other head told him '*Go*'. Before he could give it any more thought, he found himself on his feet and trailing after her red heels after throwing a couple fifties on the table for the bill.

Picking up his pace, he finally caught up with her once she had rounded the corner of the café and had stopped in her tracks in front of the alley between the café and an indie author bookstore. As he reached out to touch her shoulder, she rounded on him. It was the sad yet determined look in her eyes that stopped him cold.

His hand was still stretched out to her as their eyes locked, it was then that he noticed the strange wind that ruffled the golden hairs on top of her head just before the unmistakable 'crack' sound reached him.

Years of training and combat experience had him tackling his ex-fiancé to the ground behind the protection of a nearby vehicle and covering her slender form with his broader one before he could even process what had happened. Time slowed. His vision tunneled. Once he assured himself that the vehicle on his right would provide ample cover from the sniper, he worked to brush Veronica's locks from her face as she reached up to cradle his cheek in her palm.

"That was... too close," she whispered. Her skin was white, and her eyes swirling pools that he was getting lost in to assure himself that she was alive, in his arms, and unharmed.

As their senses returned them to the present, he felt her fumbling at his waistline. He followed what he thought her lead was and reached for the weapon in his holster as he sat back on his heels and scanned around to secure the area. He couldn't identify a threat in the immediate area. Thanks to the silenced crack of the rifle, the bystanders in the café were not aware of the life-or-death situation unfolding outside their windows.

After scanning the area, he cast another glance at Veronica with the expectation she'd be combat ready next to him and ready to support his next move. Instead, he found her standing and staring off in the general direction the round must have come from - the roof of the only five-story building on an adjacent street.

Fear rode hard on top of his anger, "Veronica! Have you lost your fucking mind?" He lunged for her and she side stepped him easily.

"I'm leaving, Bowie," her heels clicked as she began to stride away, "I recommend getting to your team."

His heart was thundering in his chest, almost drowning out her words. Comprehension was out of his grasp as he watched the sway of her hips as she walked away from him.

"Veronica? Wha—" before he could articulate his confusion and concern for her, his phone started to emit a cry for his attention. He knew from the ringtone alone that it was Guru and that he would only be reaching out directly if there was something that demanded his immediate attention.

Detachedly, he reached for the phone in his back pocket, *'Can this night get any more FUBAR?"*

CHAPTER 5
BETTING MEN

2300hrs

26 August 2030

P1O. Youngblood, Mitch "Heavy"

They had been playing the parts of First Class Privates that had gotten busted for insubordination thoroughly enough to be put on a shit detail of unloading aircraft at night. Two hours had passed in that way. Heavy was enjoying himself. He'd secretly enjoyed drama class in high school, and his own natural humor was making the role come easily to him.

His team leader was struggling. He had to elbow Kale when he looked ready to tell a too young-for-his-rank with a dick-size to match Sergeant where to shove it a time or two. That young-gun Sergeant had wanted to smoke them, just for shits and giggles. They had ended up outdoing the eager Sergeant by hitting a hundred pushups during an early attempted put down session with ease. He had left them alone after that, looking for easier targets, they were sure.

The two of them were currently sitting on a jersey barrier next to their assigned hanger as they waited for the next plane to land for them to unload. The lamppost's dying light flickered above their heads as mosquitoes harassed the air around them.

"I swear, on Lady Guadalupe, if I have to do this for one more hour I'm going to lose my shit on these fuckers."

Heavy did his best to smother a laugh at his friend. Once upon a time, Kale wasn't wound so tightly, but even then, he'd had little patience for military personnel who either abused their position of power or had no respect for the uniform they wore. On an air force runway, during mid-shift, they were surrounded by the two groups that got under Kale's skin the deepest.

Heavy was taking the piss at his friend's expense whenever he could get the chance, because it was the most animated he had seen him be in quite some time. By flexing his legs out in front of him he did his best to control the laughter bubbling up in his throat as he responded, "You know boss, that the likelihood of all of us completing this type of investigative mission in one night is slim as a hair on a donkey's ass?"

Kale redirected his gaze from observing the going-ons of the airstrip to shoot him one of the most expressive looks he'd ever seen the man shoot anyone, "Hair, on a donkey's ass? Really? You and Twigs and your country-ass expressions," then, turning his attention back to the air-deck, he added, "We aren't the types for these missions… I'm worried about the Sergeant Major. This is not the type of mission he would normally ask of us. I think he is too close to this."

The familiar sound of a turbine engine in the distance was their first warning of an approaching aircraft, "Well 'course he is, how can you blame him? Look, I know this isn't our usual octane level mission, but if Guru's intel is right—and it usually is—we could be dealing with something a lot more dangerous than any mission before this one." He stood up then, shook out his stiffening limbs, and realized how eager he was to get to the gym once their shift was over.

"Sí. But that doesn't mean I have to like it… it's hard to believe that someone in JSOC is bringing in WMD materials on our own military flights though. Are we sure he isn't crossing some wires? How did this leak go from intel on locations of next-gen warfare to flying in shit on midnight cargo craft?" Kale shook his head vigorously, "Seriously Heavy, something isn't lining up here… but I can't put my finger on it."

Heavy nodded his head in agreement. It was all things he had analyzed himself. What they were encountering was sometimes the worst part about investigative missions like this. It was like getting a single piece of a thousand-piece puzzle and having to figure out not only where to find the next piece, but what shape that piece was. It sure was a tall order. Often waiting for that puzzle piece to reveal itself was the only option.

He turned back to Kale as he pushed off the barrier and flicked his chin in the direction of the hanger, "Lets Charlie-Mike," said Kale. "I see some new faces and, judging by the patches, they may be who we are waiting on."

"Bet KP duty for a month this shit is not going to be locked down in one night," he muttered, falling into step next to Kale and noting that the aircraft he had heard in the distance was close to landing now.

"I'll take that bet, 'cause for my sanity this charade needs to end tonight."

CHAPTER 6
ROOKIE MISTAKES

0033hrs

27 August 2030

SGM. Post, Jerry Bowie

Jerry followed Guru's directions and found the derelict 1950s water treatment plant at the backend of Fort Bragg's ranges. It had not been used since the base upgraded its water systems a few decades ago, but someone had clearly taken advantage of its square footage and isolation. As he got within a half mile of the facility, he cut his headlights and duct taped his running lights so that they did not give away his approach.

The deep night seemed to swallow him and his truck up as he slowly navigated along the unmaintained road until he located Kale's similarly treated SUV parked just outside the facility. It was concealed behind a crumbling guard shack that was a relic from a different time in military history.

He was still reeling from the sniper attack on Veronica, and how she had literally just walked it off without any explanation to him. On top of that there was deep-seated concern that the attempted assassination had something to do with his investigation. The idea that it may have been a warning to back off clung to him. He felt sick with the thought that he had put her in danger by going straight to her with his inquiry. It had taken Guru explaining that Kale and Heavy had not only identified the soldiers collecting unidentified items from the late night C130 shipments but had also followed them to what appeared to be their base of operations, for him to prioritize their last-minute mission over his concerns about Veronica.

Hoping that nailing them would eliminate the threat to Veronica, he snapped out of his confusion from the events and double-timed it over to join his men. A plan was forming in his mind to take Veronica aside after all this was over and beg her to take him back, but also explain to her how stupidly she had acted after the attack. Something about her reaction still rubbed him wrong. As a seasoned soldier, surely, she knew better than to expose herself to a sniper for another shot.

Jerry tried to push thoughts of her out of his head as he slipped out of his vehicle and closed the door gently, pressing his weight against it till it snicked shut. Training told him he needed to be alert and ready for the mission at hand. He dropped into a crouch and made his way over to the rally point Guru had described to him. Off to the right of the guard shack and behind a concrete barrier was where he would find his men waiting for him by an opening they had made in the rusted fence. As he approached them, he saw Kale and Heavy turn in unison and level their carbines in his general direction before dropping the muzzles as they identified him.

"Took you long enough, must have been one hell of a 'not date'," Heavy whispered, as he handed him a vest, helmet, comm set, and fully loaded M4 with three extra magazines.

His scowl was lost in the darkness, and he kept his retort to himself as it would have only affirmed Heavy and Kale's suspicions. Plus, he couldn't have explained if he wanted to. He was still trying to understand what exactly had happened that evening and knew that if he was going to get through this night in one piece he had to forget about Veronica and focus on the mission at present.

Kale turned to him as he began to put his gear on and briefed him in a no-nonsense tone of voice, "We followed the two from the airfield.

They were the ones who had cleared the deck when the last cargo plane came in. We observed them unloading three wooden crates, then passing something to the Chief on Deck, and loading the cargo up in that van. We've identified one other vehicle on the other side of the complex. Guru can't get us any schematics or video though, as the building is pre-anything."

"Best point of entry?" Post shot back, as he ran a weapons check on his M4 and situated his gear in a way that fit him better.

"This side of the building. There's an old bay door, half closed, from what we can tell from poking around. The bulk of the group is on the far end so we shouldn't run into anything on entry," Kale rattled off, then thumbed his comm into his ear, "Check."

Heavy, Guru, and himself all clicked their throat mics to confirm they could hear him. "How many did you identify?"

Shifting his weight to angle his body back towards the dark, deteriorating building complex, he responded, "At least one by the entrance closest to the vehicles, and two to three in what Guru thinks is the old treatment part of the plant." His voice wavered with the last bit of information.

"That concerns you?" Post slapped a magazine into the rifle's mag-well.

"I don't like it." Kale replied.

"Explain."

It was rare to see Kale waver on a mission, and it meant that they should all take extra care with their execution of it. Kale huffed, "I've been in old treatment plants like this growing up, the water containment areas usually contain deep pits, either circles or swimming pool shapes, embedded deep in the ground. On a good day, they are a tipping hazard, but on a mission at night, with potential for incoming fire, they would be death traps if we had our back to one, or—Dios forbid—fell into one."

"Add in a derelict building on top of all that… all right." Post sat still for a moment, analyzing the building and the information Kale had provided. "Our mission is to find out what's in those crates, if it's related to some next-gen warfare, or—worst case—WMDs. If that's the case, then we need to know, now. Also…" he paused and looked at Kale and Heavy. In the dim light offered by a crescent moon he could just barely make out their silhouettes and the angles of their faces, but he knew without a doubt he had their full attention. "We have to take them alive, but they will not return that courtesy."

"Horse-Mahogany," Heavy cursed out in his Texas way, and Kale held his breath for a moment until he stated flatly, "I don't relish the idea of killing our own, traitors or not, but this doesn't put the odds in our favor here."

Post nodded, "I said don't kill them… doesn't mean you can't cap them in a non-lethal area. I'd rather not kill any of them, but they picked the wrong side this go round, and your lives matter more to me than theirs. Ultimately, we just need one of them to tell us who they are leaking info to, what they've told them so far, and find out what's in those crates and secure them."

He flipped the selector switch on his carbine from semi-auto to single shot and heard his men follow his lead. "Call it, Kale."

"We'll do this guerrilla style, then. Aim to separate them and take them out by hand if possible. Remember, all of them are possibly special ops as well so hand to hand may not be as easy, nor as quiet as we'd like. If you cause a ruckus, call it out, end the fight and get out of the line of fire as the others will be running towards it. Post, you'll start with the man by the vehicles, Heavy and I will go in the back and try to separate them and take them out. Guru is on standby, but there's really nothing he can do for us since the building isn't connected to shit."

Post agreed with Kale's call. There really was no perfect way to execute such a last-minute mission, but the stakes were too high to let the players stay in motion any longer than they already had been. A shudder coursed through him at the idea of some unknown, next-gen tech or WMD just sitting in that building with a potential target inside the U.S. and how it was all unfolding so close to D.C.

It only took him a moment to get from the rally point to the far end of the old treatment plant. Now that he was closer to it, he assumed that the only reason the thing hadn't caved in entirely was thanks to its old brick and cinder block construction. He slowed his pace and began placing each booted foot carefully, analyzing in the dim light from the moon what he was stepping on. Glass shards littered the ground and threatened to give away his approach with a single misstep.

As he neared the area where the vehicles were stationed, the ground under his feet became a mosaic of interlaced red brick. Resisting the urge to admire the craftsmanship someone nearly a hundred years ago had put into it, he continued. After another minute of careful, cat-like movements, he found a pony wall that separated what turned out to be a sidewalk encompassing the building and the second loading bay he was looking for.

Unlike its sister on the other side, this bay was fully functioning and operable. He watched as a burly, short man with a bald head leaned against one of the trucks and nursed a cigarette. His body language screamed boredom. Post knew that boredom meant carelessness.

Taking a moment to take in the surroundings, he found himself a path that cut behind the vehicles and his target. He just had to hope that the man didn't move before Kale and Heavy sent the signal that they were inside and ready to act. Luck was on his side. Just as he found his way behind the man, he heard two clicks in his comm. Kale and Heavy were in position and ready to engage. He clicked his own comm once to give them the go ahead, then carefully slung his rifle across his back so it wouldn't bang into the vehicles on either side of him.

Every step felt like an eternity as he placed each booted foot, methodically rolling his arches to minimize the impact of his heels striking the bare brick. All while remaining within the shadow cast by the truck and the spotlight behind it. One more step. That was all he needed to place himself fully behind his target. As he took it, the man flicked his cigarette away, "Why am I always on fucking guard duty?"

Post couldn't help himself as he retorted, "Let me relieve you then."

Before his enemy could react, he had him in a tight headlock and had pulled him into the relative concealment offered by the vehicles. Knowing the man had musculature and youth on his side, he wasted no time in wrapping his legs around the man's waist and twisting to the right. The man's face was soon pressed into the ground and his arms pinned between it and his body. Less than thirty seconds was all it took for him to go limp. but Post maintained his hold for an additional five seconds to assure himself that the man wasn't trying to fake him out. Rolling the man over onto his back, Post quickly checked for a pulse, verified he was still breathing, then flexi-cuffed his hands and feet together, before zip-tying him to the truck's running board.

After clicking his comm three times to let his men know that he had neutralized the first target, he began to make his way into the building. Time had slowed considerably for him in that moment of action, though it had only lasted ninety-six seconds. As he wondered how his men were doing, he heard three clicks through his earpiece, *'Good, two down, now two to three more left and we can figure out what kind of shit Veronica has gotten herself into.'* Yes, he had thought Veronica wasn't capable of being a traitor, and he still believed that with every fiber of his being. But that sniper earlier had been aiming for her, possibly to scare her off the investigation. He knew she had some part to play in all this. The question was, what role?

Moving past the loading bay placed him in an expansive room with brick archways to each side and overlooking what must have been the treatment bays. Post saw that Kale's concern was well founded, as the pits were easily two meters in height and he didn't see any easy way out of them. His eyes settled on the corner of the room closest to him, where three large flood lamps illuminated the brilliant red brick façade of what must have been the old control room, though it had long since been stripped of anything valuable by scrap thieves.

The only thing filling it out now were roughhewn cargo boxes. Sitting on one and standing by another were two men. One he placed immediately as a member of Veronica's unit. He was the one that'd leveled that disdainful gaze at him after his verbal trade with her. So, they were part of her unit… but did she know? The only way he would find out was by asking, but first he'd need to separate them from their

M4s resting along a box between them. Sneaking closer, he heard snatches of their conversation, which was not hard as they were practically yelling at each other.

"… I set this shit up, so the bigger cut goes to me."

"Bull… she would be on to us if it… for him…"

The man sitting on the crate threw his arms up in clear frustration, "Who is… we've never seen this person."

Post realized his mistake just as the two men reeled on him without warning when he was just ten yards away. He had committed the cardinal sin for operators – he had a personal stake in this mission.

In his eagerness to clear, or condemn, Veronica based on their conversation, he had focused more on what they were saying than where he was stepping. The crunch of shattered glass underfoot had been the only noise the trained men had needed to hear to put them on high alert.

It was a rookie mistake, and one that could cost him his life.

As he raised his weapon to level on the man nearest to him, he hesitated. His second rookie mistake.

If he killed the man, he may not get answers to his questions about Veronica. If he did not kill him, he wouldn't live long enough to care about the concerns of the living. His fallen brothers and sisters would be welcoming him to Valhalla.

Then came his third and final rookie mistake. As his reactions became muddled by concerns that did not belong on a battlefield, he froze with indecision. Failure ensued. A failure to move to cover, failure to fire his weapon to kill, and failure to prioritize his life over an answer to a question he valued more than it in that moment.

He registered in slow motion as the soldier drew his sidearm and leveled it on him. *'Three strikes… will she miss me?'*

"Hey Pendejo!"

A shouted expletive in Spanish ricocheted through the room. The sound of a single shot followed it, shattering the strange hyper awareness of time that was the side effect of adrenaline. Before he even registered what was happening he had fallen two meters into the empty water treatment vat that had been behind him. Only a pile of garbage at its bottom and his helmet had saved him from more serious trauma.

Barely clinging to consciousness, he noted that each breath he took hurt like hell. Pain was good, it told him he was alive. He knew the shooter's aim must have been thrown off by Kale's shout, so he wasn't immediately killed, but he knew he had been shot. They were too close for him to have missed completely. Post had felt the impact in his hip. The impact and his own, admittedly delayed, response to move out of the line of fire had led him to his current predicament.

As his breathing leveled out, he began to register the sounds of shots being exchanged. The empty expanse of the brick building made the sounds ricochet in all directions, causing it to seem like the four-person gunfight was taking place between entire battalions on the shores of Tripoli.

His earpiece crackled, "Yo, old man!" Guru screamed at him through the tiny device, concern thick in his voice.

Victor "Guru" West was the only person in Jerry's life that could get away with calling him that. He had known Victor since he was in diapers, so he often let the nickname slide. Ignoring the pain radiating from his hip and back, he finally mustered the will to heave himself off the trash and lean against the side of the pit to look for an egress point. He was dead to rights if the enemy above him found him here. He needed to get out, while Kale and Heavy had their attention.

"Can't get rid of me that easy, son..."

"Oh, thank the pagan Gods, Allah, and fucking Ares!"

He chuckled at Victor's prayer, he was a man of all faiths, yet none at the same time, "Thought you didn't have eyes?"

There was a clatter of keystrokes as Guru responded tersely, "I had Heavy and Kale duct tape their phones to their chest, now make like a banana and split! They can't cover you for long."

"And why aren't they yelling at me instead of you?"

"Just move, Grandpa! Straight and to your right, there looks to be something there you can use to get out of that hole."

"Understood. Kale, Heavy, keep their attention I'll loop around on their six."

He didn't wait for their acknowledgement as he tried to move as swiftly as possible across the tank. His hip screamed at him, warning him that he needed to assess his injuries, but getting out of that pit took precedence.

Some discarded pallets made for a perfect impromptu ladder. As he scrambled up and cleared the edge, he dove behind the closest wall, unsure if he had been seen.

A glance at the area he had been in before his fall confirmed that the men who had fired on him were still sending rounds down the length of the room to a corner so dark, he couldn't even make out the walls. They either hadn't noticed his escape or had assumed he'd died from the fall.

"Start aiming high, and I swear if you hit me, I'll haunt your asses!" Two clicks of a comm mic was all he needed, to know that the gunfire had been redirected and that they had given him the opening he needed.

Before they could realize that they were no longer under direct fire, Post had walked up behind the one he had labeled as Mr. Disdain and drilled the barrel of his rifle in the small gap at the base of his skull.

"How about we call it a night, eh boys?" He eyed the other soldier who watched the scene in front of him, weighing whether he had enough time to take out Post before he could shoot his partner. After a couple tense seconds, reason won out and the man dropped his gun and held his arms up high, signally an end to the fight.

"Now, how about we have a civilized fucking debrief?"

CHAPTER 7
HOW A HEART BREAKS

0252hrs
27 August 2030
SGM Post, Jerry

There were not enough cuss words in the world to sum up how he felt at that moment. He knew he needed to slow down by how his truck was tipping precariously in each turn. His adrenaline filled mind knew he was playing a dangerous game, but he had only one objective at that point and he was focused entirely on getting to her.

The men at the treatment plant weren't who they were after. Those shitbags were involved in the black market and moving priceless antiques that their counterparts overseas had lifted and smuggled onto homebound craft. He had left Heavy and Kale to clean up the mess as Guru contacted the base's CID department and local FBI unit. It was messy and would surely not be good optics for JSOC. But it wasn't what they had been looking for.

They did, however, tell him one thing that provided a partial, yet unwelcome, answer to his questions. He thought back to that brief exchange with the men at the plant.

"The first Sergeant? Yeah, she found out about our operations awhile back." Mr. Disdain had said, with enough scorn to confirm Post had labeled him with a fitting nickname. He had been pacing in front of the bound men as they interrogated them while waiting on CID and FBI to show up on their own time. He had stopped cold in his tracks at Disdain's remark, though.

"And she did what?" Post snapped at him. Mr. Disdain had frozen then, sensing danger in Post's sudden change. "Well, the lot of us knew she had some gig on the side, so we told her if she let us get our cut, we'd let her keep hers."

"Oh? Exactly what 'gig' did she have?" He got down into the man's face then, his anger bubbling over.

"We didn't know. Just knew it had something to do with that ancient MP3 thing of hers. She'd have it one week, like an addiction, on her always, then it would be gone for a week. It was her modern-day Edward Snowden routine. That's all we knew."

Once the words had sunken in, he'd double timed it back to his truck, ripped the tape off the headlights, threw it into gear, and was rushing back to base.

No, they weren't who they were after. In truth, the mole, the traitor, the person who shared classified secrets that were getting innocent U.S military men and women killed was his ex-fiancé, Veronica fucking Moody.

He punched the roof of the truck. "GOD DAMN IT, VERONICA!" He screamed her name so hard his throat was left raw.

He was hurtling to her place, in the family housing section of Fort Bragg, but he had a feeling she wasn't going to be home. The pieces were all falling into place as he played each moment, each word, over in his mind.

Then a thought clung to him and made him ache more than even knowing of the depth of her betrayal to her country did, '*Had it all— the flirting, the kiss, all of it—been a ruse to keep me off her trail long enough for her to get away?*'

Rationally, he knew she wasn't going to answer his call. But he had to try. He had to know. As he pressed the call button, he knew he was acting irrationally, but couldn't find a single ounce of give-a-damn to care about it. Later, he would look back on that moment and realize he had committed another cardinal sin of warfare - falling in love with the enemy.

"Bowie…"

Her name on his lips over his speakers shocked him so much that he almost wrecked the truck. A squeal of the tires and he was back on blacktop, "Veronica! What the damn hell is going on?! Where ar—"

"Bowie, if you don't stop yelling at me, so help me, I'll hang up this phone and you'll never get the answers you want so fucking badly!"

Her voice cut him to the core. There was an edge to it he'd never heard before. Somehow, he knew that this was a different Veronica from the one he had promised to marry five years ago.

"I'll take your silence as confirmation you are going to listen," she hissed, then he heard her take a shaky breath and bit back the retort building in his chest.

"I am the mole you are looking for, Bowie, but I'm no traita', regardless of what you think. I am loyal to my country, Bowie, but being a mother will always come first."

The truck slowed under him, "V.."

"They've had a man on John-Masters for months now. He is my only weak point, and they found it and applied pressure. I was supposed to make one last drop tonight, then they were going to leave us both alone. The sniper was supposed to spook you to get you off my tail. Then he deliberately put that bullet close enough to scalp me. That was a message to me that I'd displeased them. It's why I handed the drop to you. What's on that Zune is the last piece of the puzzle they are looking for…"

"V, you didn't…"

"How can you be fucking Black Ops and not know when a woman puts the equivalent of a small brick in your pocket?" She snickered, but he could hear the unshed tears in her voice.

"I need you to promise me something, Bowie…"

"You are in no position to be asking favors, V," he growled, "Stay where you are, I'm coming to get you."

She laughed at his naiveté, "Bowie, unless you grow wings you aren't catching me. It's too late for me, love. I'll be an enemy of the U.S once what is on that Zune is decrypted."

He was finding it increasingly hard to care about the road in front of him as he felt his heart ripping in his chest. This was different than five years ago. This felt final, in a way it hadn't before, "What's the favor?"

"I think John will be safe with me on the run… but please, Bowie, please carry on keeping tabs on him and maybe, one day, tell him why I did what I did. The greatest love in the world is that of a mother…"

Slamming his palm against the steering wheel, he snapped at her, "Don't talk like that, come back here and I'm sure we can get you a plea deal or something, but not if you run!"

It was no use. The resignation was clear in her voice, even as the connection started to crackle, "Listen to me, Bowie, this organization, not my government, is who I am running from. They are something we have never been up against. They have people everywhere, and their hands in everything. Do not trust anyone. They can get to anyone, and they control everyone with influence, stay alive lov—" the connection faded then, and the signal fell out completely.

"V? Veronica!" his breath came in heaves. He felt as if he was falling into that pit all over again. This time he didn't think he would survive the fall.

Driving wasn't even a conscious thing he was doing anymore. It was like another person had the wheel, as he analyzed everything that had led up to that moment and replayed their conversation. Upon reaching the point when she'd mentioned having put something in his pocket, he took one hand off the wheel and searched himself.

He pulled out her Zune. Instead of being the perfect black brick it had been, he found its screen shattered with a 9mm round nestled in the center of a spider web pattern. The thing had saved his life.

He had been so caught up in the firefight that he had completely forgotten about feeling the impact of the round and checking for an injury.

Her last gift to him not only saved his life but could also–with

Guru's help–hopefully shed light on who'd threatened the lives of Veronica and her son thoroughly enough for her to betray the country she loved.

His attention in that moment was so focused on the device in his hand that it took him a whole three seconds to realize that there was a set of headlights to his left, where only trees should have been. It would be the last rookie mistake he'd make.

0302hrs
27 August 2030
UNKNOWN

The brother of Hades causally stepped out of his commandeered, up-armored Humvee. As he rounded the front end, a quick glance confirmed that the only visible indication of the military vehicle having been in a collision was some black transferred paint. The next unit inspection of the vehicles would bring it to light, but no one would even think to tie it to tonight's events.

He casually continued his march towards the side of the cliff that he had just pushed the truck off of. Yawning, he checked his watch and winced at the time. Soon, the on-duty MPs would be heading back to Bragg for shift change and 'she' would come this way.

He pulled out his phone and glanced at the hacking software that showed him where all the patrol vehicles were based on their blue force trackers. He punched in her car's identifier and found her right where he expected her to be - camped out on an empty range just a couple miles down from his location. It had given him just enough space and time to complete his mission.

As he peered over the dark graveled edge of the drop off, he could just make out the outline of the vehicle thanks to its headlights that had miraculously managed to remain functional during the violent tumble down the hillside and now flashed an SOS that its computer systems dictated after detecting the crash. This was a safety feature he found useful for his needs at that moment. The job was done well enough for his purposes and would satisfy Hades' request.

The sound of an engine picking up speed cut through the trees around him. He expected she was on her way back to base and spun on his boot heel. Curious to see if the Sergeant Major would be found, and how things would play out, he returned to his Humvee before making his way to an area with higher elevation that would provide him with a clearer line of sight. As he settled in to see what events his plan would set in motion, he wondered if he could let go of her when the time came.

Gazing out into the night, entrusting that dark silent mistress alone with his secrets, he said solemnly, "It's easier to live a convenient lie, than a painful truth."

EPILOGUE: BEGINNINGS

A voice called out to him. It was a woman's voice. She was calling his name. '*Veronica?*'

He struggled against the inky blackness that tugged at him and whispered of blissful oblivion. Sheer will was the only thing that propelled Sergeant Major Post to respond to the voice. Tossing his head to chase away the blackness, he tried to regain full consciousness.

As his eyes flicked open, finally responding to his commands, he saw her. '*Not Veronica...*'

This unknown woman was asking him something, but it was so hard to understand her for some reason. Finally, he comprehended she was worried about him, she was an MP, she was asking if he was hurt. And yes, he was hurt, shattered in fact, but no medical personnel in the world could help the pain he felt in his chest.

He tried to answer her, but the moment he attempted to draw breath into his lungs they rejected it. A coughing fit overtook him as he struggled to breathe around a torrent of what he knew was his own blood.

"Fuck!"

Her crass and spontaneous outburst grabbed his attention, and he smiled inwardly. All soldiers, early on, master the use of the all-powerful word 'fuck' and he couldn't think of a better time to use it. He was well and truly fucked. Though Post was no stranger to such fuckery. He had danced with death more often than any man should, either personally or while screaming at it to fuck-off by a friend's side, often in vain.

The young MP next to him was putting what felt to be every bit of her weight into his wounded side in a vain attempt to staunch the bleeding. It brought his fading attention back to her.

She was a beautiful soldier, and clearly a capable MP, and was determined to fight for his life even though he had already accepted his fate. His heart was already shredded, what more could death do to him? He knew his warriors would be in good hands, he just hoped that John would be okay without him.

Death was waiting with open arms, and he would no longer resist its embrace. He was at peace with it. Though, as he examined the soldier next to him, he did feel remorse for her.

Would his be the first death in her arms? Would she blame herself?

He suddenly felt the need to make sure she knew that none of this was her fault. He knew he had made one too many rookie mistakes that night and had been lucky to have made it this far, but it had all caught up to him now.

The Humvee that struck him was nowhere to be found, and he suspected it wouldn't be. If he had ever been a betting man, he knew he would have gambled that it was tied to the organization Veronica had tried to warn him about. He felt a bit peeved at not being able to tie up that loose end, but who was he to complain now?

"You are not going to die. I'm going to get you out of this ditch, but you need to fight. You got that, damn it?" Her voice cut through his thoughts and acceptance of death. He admired her spirit; she said it like she really thought he was going to survive this.

'Okay, lil' MP. I'll fight for you. But unless you have a miracle hidden in that holster of yours, you and I both are fighting a losing battle...'

~~~ The story continues in **'Virgil Team'** ~~~
~~~

DEAR READER:

I hope you enjoyed Post's story and if you haven't read 'Virgil Team', please remember that this short story is a prequel to the events in the first chapter of my debut novel!

As always, thank you for reading and I'd be very grateful and appreciative of any time you take to write a review on Amazon and Goodreads! Reviews like yours help indie authors like me be found by other readers.

Don't forget to follow me via my website and social media for updates and character art!

May Virgil guide you!
Bonnie

P.S. Special shout out to PatriotWrites for her support of fellow veteran authors, and her book club that inspired me to write Post's story!

ABOUT THE AUTHOR

Bonnie Blevins was born and raised in Culpeper, Virginia. Growing up, she was an active part of her community and enjoyed volunteering at a horseback riding center for disabled children. A lifelong aspiration to join the military culminated in her joining the U.S Army when she turned seventeen. During her service, she started writing in earnest and unwittingly laid the foundations for Virgil Team. At the time, it was lovingly labeled 'Timewaster' on her computer, but after suffering an injury that resulted in her service ending earlier than planned, she found new aspirations as a writer. When she isn't writing, Bonnie enjoys horseback riding, photography, and video games.

https://authorbonnieblevins.wixsite.com/bonnie-blevins-books

Follow Bonnie Blevins on:

facebook.com/BonBlev

x.com/BonnieBlev17

instagram.com/BonnieBlevins117

goodreads.com/Bonnie_Blevins